# The Crimson Suitor
# Demon Hunter Prelude
# Tim Niederriter

Snowstorms moved out of the west over Chos Valley, leaving every twisted tree and rocky slope covered in white when Deckard Hadrian arrived at Keep Nothem.

The keep had been built in the final days of the conquest, over a thousand years ago. Deckard remembered the ancient walls from his first journey north as a boy. In the intervening time, the walls had been expanded and built higher with wooden structures. The underlying white stone of solid Eshnishi craft could not be improved upon by human skill. When the new human-made walls began to crumble and the wood that crowned the older fortifications rotted to dust the work of the demon kin would only shine brighter.

Deckard flew on the cold wind, face wrapped in a cowl. His robe moved like silk around him. The heavy garment's blessed metal kept most of him warm and the hood and gloves served the rest. The wind carried him, wingless, over the steep rooftops of black wood. He landed in the snowy courtyard. His sleek boots left small traces in the snow, quickly covered by blustering wind. He folded his gloved hands into the sleeves of his burnished robe as he walked toward the inner gate.

After more than three centuries, the head of the Nothem family had seen the need to summon him.

1

"Who goes there?" asked a warmly-clad guard standing just inside the bars of the gate.

"I am Deckard Hadrian, here at the summons of your mistress."

"Lord Hadrian?" Eyes lit up in the gloomy afternoon light. "So soon?"

"I can travel quickly when I'm needed."

Deckard pulled away the scarf and cowl covering his mouth. Most people would recognize him thanks to Mercy's tarot, which usually depicted his sharp features, smooth skin, shock of dark hair, and green eyes accurately. As his first teacher once told him, Hadrian's face stood as a perfect example of a Dominion man. Dark hair and pale eyes were more common in the valley when he was young.

These days, the heritage of the Palavians predominated, with lighter hair and darker eyes, a reverse of his own features. No doubt most mortals did not notice the change, given only brief lives.

"It is cold out here, as you likely noticed, friend," said Deckard.

"Of course, Lord Hadrian."

The guard hauled on a rope to raise the bars. Deckard stepped into the narrow gateway with the heavily dressed man.

"Thank you."

The guard bowed, suddenly seeming nervous. He turned toward the inner door. His bare hands fumbled with a brass key. He raised it to the lock but shivers ran through him. The key slipped from his fingers. Deckard caught the key in his glove before it could hit the floor.

"I apologize, lord," the guard said quickly.

"No need, friend." Deckard set the key in the lock. "Shame on whoever sent you outside lacking gloves."

The man's eyes brightened over his scarf. Deckard pushed the door inward with a creak of wood. Then he pulled off both his dark woolen gloves, folded the key in them, and handed the small bundle to the guard.

"Make use of those for now," he said.

"T-thank you!"

Deckard nodded to the guard, then stepped past him and into the keep.

* * *

The seat hall of Keep Nothem was lit by bright torches in the sconces, except around the ornate dire throne at the far end from where Deckard entered. The dire throne gleamed with shifting pulses of pale light from sprites contained within the demon bones that made up the chair. That light illuminated the woman sitting before him as Deckard walked down the carpet at the center of the hall.

A handful of courtiers and knights stood at attention for the widowed lady of the Nothem family.

Deckard threw back his hood, casting water from what little snow had stuck to the sleek black cloth onto the carpet behind him.

He strode to lowest of the three tiers around the dire throne, at the apex of which sat the lady of the house.

Lady Saylese Dire-Nothem regarded him with cool eyes, brown like a Palavian's, though her hair was black like that of the Dominion people. A delicate nose and high cheekbones made her face a striking one. Small laugh lines at the corners of her lips deepened slightly as he gazed at her. A dark-green gown hugged her lithe frame closely despite the winter chill present in the seat hall.

Deckard bowed to her, as this was her house.

"Dire Lady, I rode the white storm here at your request. I take it you did not summon me idly."

"That is true, lord of demon hunters," said the lady.

"Alas, mine is a lonely title. I take it that title is what prompted your summons?"

"Unfortunately, that is true, Lord Hadrian."

She stood up from her gently glowing seat and motioned to the hangers-on to leave the room. Everyone except a gray-haired woman bearing a sword, and a young man with the high black collar of a parson, hurriedly left the hall.

When they were gone, the lady of the keep walked to the top of the steps. Deckard would have towered over her had she descended to stand on his level. Her hair gleamed, patterned by shiny silver chain-links dangling around her ears. Her two retainers flanked her, the sword-bearing woman on the right, and the young man on the left.

"These are my closest retainers," said the lady. She motioned to the swords-woman. "My sword servant Jaska." She nodded to the young parson. "And the family cleric, Andrew Tybir Reen, of Mercy's holy orders."

"I take it they already know the situation?" Deckard said.

Saylese took a deep breath and smoothed the hem of her dress with her hands.

"Regrettably, I don't think I truly understand what is happening. The Crimson Suitor is—was a mere legend to me until three days ago."

"You were wise enough to summon me." Deckard smiled. "The Crimson Suitor courts women, usually those bound or soon to be bound to another... He is a renegade even among his kind."

"Indeed?" Saylese frowned. "You're knowledge of demons is, of course, substantial, Lord Hadrian."

Deckard nodded. "The Suitor begins with polite letters. He may seem a simple paramour, but his advances quickly become violent if not reciprocated. And if reciprocated..."

"No need to worry about that," said Saylese. She motioned to the painting of a man behind the dire-seat. "It will take more than flowery words to sway my loyalty to my lost love."

"Sir Joliet was a lucky man. I met him during his final campaign." Deckard's gaze captured the painting, a young man with pale Palavian hair and a strong jawline. "He was a great warrior, my lady."

"And a true lover," she said, sounding distant. She coughed into her fist. "How does one ward off these unwanted advances, my lord?"

"In all my years of hunting demons, I have encountered the Suitor only twice before during his pursuit of a bride. More often I have been too late."

Saylese bit her lip. "You mean—"

"I have sought restitution from him for the loss of virtue, but he is not a kind demon. He does worse to his brides, things I cannot undo."

"I see. How did you stop him in the past?" Saylese looked up at his face, hope written in her eyes.

A hope he did not want to dash at once, as he should have. Deckard hesitated. He wanted to be truthful, needed to be clear, but Saylese seemed all too willing to see him as a hero. After three hundred years of battling renegade demons, such respect he might have earned. Deckard opened his mouth to speak.

A voice cut him off across the hall, deep and weary.

"He failed both times," said the man approaching from the hall behind Deckard.

Deckard's heart sank. His brows bent involuntarily into a glare that made Saylese take a step back. Deckard looked over his shoulder, already recognizing the speaker from his voice.

"Parson Dane," said Saylese, face reddening, "I thought you were tutoring my son."

Virgil Silas Dane stood stark. Long white hair tied into a single long braid down his back. His black clothes and pale skin set each other off, making aged features look skeletal in the light of the torches and the dire throne.

"When I heard Lord Hadrian had arrived, I felt the need to make myself present here." Virgil folded his white-gloved hands, the brass ring wrapped around each digit chimed, almost as though their owner were sounding tiny bells. "I see I was correct to do so."

Deckard turned fully to face Virgil. At over sixty years old, Virgil always looked tired. Half his life he had spent as Deckard's enemy, on behalf of his princely master. In all the land of mercy, there might be no mage more accomplished, at least, no mortal one.

Tension pulled Deckard's limbs taut. He glared at Virgil.

"I am here on behalf of our lady. Perhaps your lord would see fit to call off his attack dog as a favor to Dire Lady Nothem."

"I know you, Hadrian. You may be immortal, but you're also predictable."

"I'll pay you this compliment. You managed to surprise me this time, Virgil. Now give way. Let me do what I came to do."

"And you are here to do what, exactly, Lord Hadrian?" Virgil's small, dark eyes flicked to Saylese's face. "My lady, I must confess, I am here not only to tutor your child. Your husband died saving my life in the east. I would serve to defend your honor in his stead."

Saylese folded her arms and looked at Deckard. Her eyes traced his jaw to his eyes, a look of which he was well aware. She said nothing for a moment, then turned to her sword servant.

"Jaska is more than able to protect my honor, Parson Dane."

"Indeed?" Virgil glanced at the younger clergyman on Saylese's other side. "Do you share this opinion, Parson Reen?"

The younger priest startled out of his attentiveness by the direct address.

"What? I mean, against any mortal, I agree, senior parson."

Virgil steepled his fingers.

"And against a demon, Reen?"

Andrew Tybir Reen stared at Virgil, halfway frozen, halfway to choking out a reply.

Virgil nodded.

"The Crimson Suitor defiles mortals. Lord Hadrian has never defeated the red beast."

Deckard felt the blood course from his heart to his head.

"Spit out your meaning, Virgil."

"I would assist in defeating the Suitor," said Virgil. "Perhaps we can act together this once, Lord Hadrian."

Saylese nodded.

"I would not turn away such an able wizard, Parson Dane. What say you, Lord Hadrian?"

"My lady..." Deckard fought with the desire to curse and sweat off the service he had offered.

Virgil was a snake, and his master only wanted to dissect Deckard. After the wars in the east, owing a debt to a deceased knight served as the sort of screen Virgil could easily make a habit of using. But he was right about one thing.

"...I confess what Virgil says about my past encounters with the Suitor is true."

"So, time to work together?" asked Saylese.

"I regret to say, I cannot. This man and I cannot trust one another."

Saylese frowned.

"Will you leave then? Night will fall in only an hour. Winter has already darkened the sky."

"In Mercy's name, Hadrian, do your duty," said Virgil.

Deckard looked over the young Parson Reen and the gray-haired Jaska. He faced Saylese.

"My lady, I have nowhere to stay this evening. I will fly southwest toward my home." Even as he spoke, Deckard planned to avoid his keep and domain completely. Where would be safe with Virgil so close behind? Likely, nowhere.

"And that's all?" Saylese shook her head.

Deckard felt his face heat up. He wished he could ever grow a real beard to conceal some of the color.

"My apologies, Dire Lady Nothem."

She raised her hand, palm facing Deckard. Her pale fingers looked delicate, frail in the warm light. Overcome with irritation at the dismissive gesture, Deckard reached back. He held his palm close to Saylese's.

She stepped forward. Her fingers folded around his hand, interlacing with his own. She tugged him closer.

He let her pull him in. She looked at him with cold eyes.

"He won't forgive you for this. You know it already," she said softly.

"Who won't forgive me?"

"Your brother, Lord Bode. He respects the dire families greatly."

"You live in his country. Dire lady or not, I will not stake my life on trusting Virgil or his master."

She shook her head. The corners of her mouth wrinkled with frustration. She looked past Deckard at Virgil, who stood patiently a few feet away.

"Parson Dane. Finish my son's lesson for the day, then return here."

"As you wish, Dire Lady Nothem." Virgil turned and swept out of the room. His long warm cloak flowed behind him.

"Leave us," Saylese said to her sword servant and parson.

Deckard kept his gaze on Saylese's face as the steps receded.

"I really am sorry."

"Funny enough, I doubt that."

"I fought alongside your husband. We were friends, so much as a man like me has mortal friends."

"My husband is gone," said Saylese. "But did you know we have met before, Lord Hadrian?"

"I do not remember," said Deckard.

"Neither do I, I'm afraid. My mother told me you were there at my naming."

"I haven't been to a naming in three decades. But your parents were both fine knights."

"I know, my lord."

"You can call me Deckard, my lady."

"I think because you will be departing, I would use your title."

He nodded.

"Is there anything else you want to say to me?"

"My parents told me you were brave, a knight among knights. Why are you afraid of an old man, wizard or not?"

"It's not Virgil I fear. It's Cyrus Bode."

"Lord Bode is a hundred miles from here."

"Are you sure of that? A hundred miles is not so far for an immortal."

She scowled at him as she unwrapped her fingers from his hand.

"That's all you have to say? Spread your wings and flee, Lord Hadrian."

He turned his back on her. The iron robe, usually light as a feather on his shoulders felt heavy and dead. He did not take a step.

"If I were only here to honor your husband's memory, perhaps I would." He took a deep breath. "But I see why he loved you. Still loves you, certainly, from beyond the veil."

The magic of his iron robe pulsed with fresh warmth. Deckard turned toward Saylese.

There were tears in her eyes.

"Thank you, my lord."

"Deckard," he said, "Dire Lady Nothem."

"Call me Saylese."

He nodded. "Saylese, thank you. I will defend your honor with all my abilities. Do you have the messenger who brought you the Suitor's proposal?"

"How did you know he sent a messenger?"

"He always does."

"She's in the dungeon."

"Please, show me the way there."

* * *

The moment Deckard stepped into the dungeon of Keep Nothem, the bitter stench reminded him of a different prison, in a different fortress, far away. The stench reminded him, but could not eclipse the suffering and disgust of the other prison. Where Keep Nothem's dungeon at least had a clean corridor, unspeakable things had littered the path between cells where Deckard had been jailed.

He suppressed a shudder at the memory. Here he was the interrogator, a twist of fate he had long ago adjusted to experiencing.

Deckard and Saylese followed the faintly glimmering white stone pathway through the darkness, lit by a sprite wand she carried ahead of her. The song of the mystic forms within the wand was soft in Deckard's mind but added to the eeriness of their pale glow.

"She is a villager from miles away, not from my land," said Saylese.

"Strange," said Deckard, "when the Suitor charms a messenger, he usually chooses one from nearer."

"You know many things about the Suitor."

"I wish I knew how to outwit him."

"We will find a way." Saylese reached back toward him.

Deckard avoided her hand.

"I'm sorry, Saylese."

"No, forgive me. I've heard stories about your oath to Mother Mercy. Only, you seemed afraid when we reached the dungeon. Don't think me presumptuous. I mean, an immortal... afraid?"

"But you were right." Deckard brushed his fingers against hers. "I was once imprisoned in a place far worse than this."

"You still remember it." She inhaled sharply in the cold, putrid air.

"Yes."

"May I ask where it happened?"

"Please, don't."

Her fingers touched the back of his hand.

"As you request."

They continued down the corridor to a cell where a warmly-dressed guard stood at attention, one fist to his heart.

"Dire Lady," said the guard.

She nodded to him.

"Footman, this is Lord Deckard Hadrian."

The guard turned his gaze to Deckard, unflappable.

"My lord."

"We are here to speak with the prisoner," said Saylese.

"By your will, my lady."

The guard unlocked the barred doors with one of the keys hanging from a heavy ring.

Saylese stepped into the cell. Deckard followed and then stopped at her side.

The prisoner was a young girl, probably no more than fourteen years old. Deckard's heart sounded loud in his ears as the pale-haired village girl looked up at him, eyes black but shining in the gloom. He met her gaze, trying to conceal his pity. Those who truly knew him would know the suffering of children never sat well with his heart.

Few living people knew him that well.

He folded his iron-clad sleeves.

"What is your name, girl?"

She sniffed, fighting tears. "Tia, milord."

"Do you know who I am, girl?"

"Deckard Hadrian."

"Yes," he said.

Tears crept into the girl's already-red-rimmed eyes.

"He sent a message for you as well, Deckard," Tia said.

Saylese glanced at Deckard.

"Go on," he said.

The girl gulped. "He said..." Her voice caught. When she spoke again, she sounded unnaturally deeper, more authoritative and commanding. "You cannot protect *anyone* from me, demon hunter. Cast me into the pit again, but the lady is mine."

Deckard scowled.

"The Suitor has left one of his banes within the girl as a charm."

Saylese leaned toward Deckard.

"Can she be restored?"

"I've encountered his charm before. I will draw the bane out."

He extended one hand, chill air nipping at his fingertips. The sleeve of his robe fell back, but not far enough to expose any of the burn scars on his upper arm. He took a deep breath, and then pressed his palm to the girl's forehead. He closed his eyes, listening for the bane song.

All humans in Mother Mercy's domain were born with a single sprite and a single bane at the core of their spirit. A poor villager likely would not have any others, except for that which the Suitor had left.

A dissonant note reached Deckard from within.

A single additional bane sang a song counter to the notes in the girl's heart, faint, but audible to those with the talent.

Eyes still closed, Deckard pressed the tip of his thumb to that of his index finger. He separated the two digits, drawing a sprite of his own between them in the form of a brightly shining thread. Eyes opening, he willed the thread toward the place where the renegade demon's solitary bane lurked under Tia's tongue.

Deckard removed his hand from the girl's forehead.

"Stay calm," he said. "Tia, I won't hurt you."

She nodded, tears in her eyes.

"Open your mouth."

Tia obeyed. She squeezed her eyes shut.

He sent the sprite string through the gap and then down to the tongue. His sprite found the bane at once and wrapped the end of the string around the struggling essence. Deckard tugged the string back to his palm, dragging the bane with it.

"It is done," he said.

Tia opened her eyes cautiously.

Deckard smiled at her, then turned to Saylese.

"She should be free of his influence now."

"So simple," she said. "Impressive."

"The Suitor's greatest power is his charm. He can compel any part of a human to obey his command by leaving a bane for influence. He is very good at it."

"I see." Saylese shivered and then drew the fur mantle tighter over her shoulders. "Frightening."

"It's cold here as well, my lady."

"You're right." Saylese turned to the girl. "Follow us, Tia."

Deckard raised his eyebrows.

"You adapt quickly. Most cannot separate the actions of the manipulated from the person acting them out so fast."

She smiled at him.

"Get used to me surprising you, my lord."

Deckard chuckled.

"I'll do my best."

They left the cell with Saylese offering a brief explanation to the guard. Deckard, Saylese, and Tia made their way up to the warmer halls of the keep above.

* * *

Saylese sent Tia to room with the servants until the storm passed. Deckard watched her discuss food for the girl with the head cook for a moment. She moved with elegance, graceful. He wondered what it would be like to dance with her.

In the valley, either the man or the woman could lead in most dances.

Deckard guessed Saylese was used to leading on the floor if she danced at all these days.

Still devoted to her slain husband, she had been left as widow far too young. He shook his head. Thoughts such as this would not do. He was here to protect her from the Suitor, not make advances of his own.

She turned toward him as she finished talking with the cook.

"Thank you for waiting, Deckard."

"Of course, Saylese." He enjoyed the sound of her name.

"Don't be surprised," she said. "Parson Dane and my son are finished with his tutoring for the day. They are headed our way."

"Perfect."

"I've heard you and Lord Bode have a great rivalry," she said. "But why worry over his servant?"

"I would not call myself Cyrus's rival. He is my brother in the service of Mother Mercy, but he has ambitions that require things of me I can never willingly give."

Saylese frowned but said nothing. She waved to someone to Deckard's left. He followed her gesture.

At first glance, Zadery Dire-Nothem resembled his Palavian father, Sir Joliet more than Saylese. A mop of straw-colored hair haloed his head, looking almost orange in fragments of fading sunlight from outside the arched windows. His eyes were dark, and his skin pale. He looked to be about ten years old, and small. The heavy gray jacket he wore made him look little larger.

He ran to Saylese.

"Parson Dane is a good teacher."

"My son," said Saylese to Deckard.

Deckard smiled.

"I recognized his father in his face."

"Does he not resemble Sir Joliet?" said Virgil, as he walked toward them, following Zadery. He sounded tired, but his feet remained swift despite his age.

Now, there was someone Deckard knew never danced.

Deckard felt his smile slip away as Virgil approached him and Saylese.

The lady nodded to Virgil.

"You knew him well."

"I lost many friends in the last war. Your husband was one of the most honorable." Virgil folded his hands together.

Saylese sighed.

"Any knight can fall, no matter his or her honor." She turned to Deckard. "I'm not sure if you know this, but I also trained with the blade. I might have ridden east with Joliet, but I was pregnant that spring." She put her hand gently on her son's head. "I know better than most widows how a knight can die."

Virgil nodded, his wrinkled faced solemn.

Deckard crouched down before Saylese and Zadery. The boy looked at him with a frown.

"You're the sleepless prince," said Zadery.

"An old title, but it is mine," said Deckard. "One of the ones I like better."

The last light of the winter day slipped past the high windows.

Saylese's lips curved, forming a smile, though a sad one.

"What makes you like it?" asked Zadery.

"I like it for its truth," Deckard said.

"Lord Hadrian never sleeps," said Virgil with a smirk. "Else he might not be here today."

"Lucky lucky," said Zadery with a grimace. "My mother always sends me to my chambers at sundown."

"Speaking of which," said Saylese sounding sly. "The nurse will take you there now, my young knight."

"But mother! I just met the sleepless prince!"

"I'm afraid it's for the best. Without proper sleep, you won't grow, and your spirit won't mature."

Zadery folded his arms and pursed his lips. "Fine. The nurse had better watch out. Once the parson teaches me how to curse someone, I won't be letting her put me to bed no more."

Deckard chuckled. He leaned forward, hands on his knees.

"You know when I was your age, I still slept at night."

"Why?"

"It's a secret."

"Tell me!"

"If I tell you, you need to go to bed."

"Fine. Fine. Tell me."

He smiled at the boy.

"Back then, I wasn't an immortal. I was like everyone else."

"But things changed."

"Yes, they changed."

*And in nearly three hundred fifty years, things never stopped changing.*

Deckard straightened his legs. Saylese brightened.

"Go with the nurse," she said to Zadery.

A woman approached, followed by a trio of male servants carrying goods for the kitchen. The woman guided Zadery away from Saylese, Deckard, and Virgil.

Saylese turned to Deckard.

"He's stubborn more and more often lately."

"Children grow quickly."

"Indeed they do," she said. "And quickly grow stubborn."

Virgil grunted, then frowned after the kitchen servants following the nurse and Zadery closely to the end of the dimming hallway.

"There is dissonance in their songs," he said. "I can't quite place it."

Deckard bent his ear to listen for sprites. Virgil was right, he realized. The nurse and each of the kitchen servants carried the spark of dissonance somewhere within, and not just any dissonance. Their spiritual disorder was the same as the girl in the dungeon's had been, that of the Crimson Suitor.

"They're charmed," Deckard said, his mouth feeling dry.

The nurse looked back at him, a wolfish grin on her face.

"Down, Hadrian," said Virgil, before muttering a series of incantations.

Deckard darted after the group down the hall, weaving away from the windows and ducking to give Virgil a clearer field of vision. A crackle of lightning and the smell of burning air filled the hallway. Deckard did not need to look back to know Virgil had just used his bolt gloves, as the electricity lanced over his shoulder. One of the kitchen servants jerked and fell to the floor, convulsing from the electrical discharge.

Saylese stormed after Deckard.

She looked over her shoulder at Virgil, brows bending inward.

"Don't hurt the servants, they're not the real enemy!"

The bags of flour carried by the servants fluttered to the floor. The steel of a blade glinted where one man had held it. Deckard raced toward them, summoning his string-sprites. He sent glowing lines to encircle one of the servant's legs, then tugged, dropping the man to the floor.

"Hadrian," Virgil said.

The last of the three kitchen servants raised a crossbow in both hands. He aimed at Saylese's legs, a shot that would maim but not kill.

Deckard leaped into the path of the bolt. Through the iron of his robe, he felt a dull impact. The bolt shattered into fragments of wood and its metal tip deformed.

Virgil's next lightning bolt dropped the crossbowman into convulsions.

Deckard scrambled after the nurse as she disappeared around the corner. He pivoted to pursue her, one hand raised with sprite strings dancing on his fingertips. The nurse and the boy were not there.

A giggle came from behind him.

"Easily deceived, demon hunter?" The voice of the nurse distorted, sounding more masculine.

He whirled.

The demon had resembled a woman but now appeared every inch a creature of his true nature. A humanoid figure covered in shimmering red silk clothes stood, clawed hands holding Zadery by the shoulders. Powerful feathered wings sprouted from the demon's back. The wings spread, revealing baffling patterns of shifting colors.

The voice of the Crimson Suitor spoke from pale lips behind a mask of slender bars.

"You arrived quicker than I expected, immortal." The Suitor's fist drove against Deckard's temple.

He fell to one knee.

Those pale lips curved.

"Perhaps you've gotten old after all, not to see through me at once."

Deckard's mouth formed a snarl as he looked up at the suitor.

"You're more brazen than ever, demon."

The Suitor's smile broadened, revealing sharp white teeth.

"Impatient perhaps." He glanced at Saylese. "My love awaits, Hadrian."

"Not this night, demon," said Saylese. "Not ever."

The Suitor shrugged.

"Play with my feelings if you will, my dear. Entice me. I will return for you."

He closed his fingers tight on Zadery's trembling frame, then beat his powerful wings.

Virgil raised a gloved hand, palm sparking with electrical power.

Saylese glared at the wizard.

"Not while he holds my son, parson."

Virgil grimaced but lowered his hand.

The Suitor flew over them. A flash of red and the large window at the far end of the hallway shattered.

Deckard and the others watched, helpless, as the demon winged into the winter evening.

He pulled himself to his feet.

"I'm going after them." He took a string sprite in his hand, then dropped it into Saylese's palm. "This sprite will follow me until it can reunite."

She nodded.

"I'll assemble my best. We'll be right behind you."

Deckard nodded, then began to shift his weight into the sprites that made him light as a feather. He ran to the window, then threw himself out into the blowing snowfall.

The wind bore him up at his command.

* * *

He glided after the Suitor, losing sight of the demon in the storm, but following the lines of his bane-seeking sprites. The wind was with him most of the way. He only used his sprites to alter its direction a few times before landing at a crossroads on a lower level in the valley where the sprites led him.

His arms hung at his sides. Without gloves, his hands felt the chill. His generosity punished him for the moment, but he could not simply wish and get his gloves back now. The Suitor was not at the crossroads, but a single loud bane song drew him to the center of the four roads. There, he found the decoy bane the Suitor had separated to lead him on.

Deckard cursed in frustration. The demon out in the cold would be hard to track, and in this cold, who could say how long Zadery had before he started to suffer the effects of frostbite. *Demon, you cannot mean to let that child die. I won't let it happen.*

Where would the Suitor flee? His true objective, Saylese, remained at Keep Nothem for the moment. If he struck too soon, she would be better prepared for him. The Suitor was craven at heart. Deckard knew all too well how little the demon liked to fight, despite his dangerous abilities.

Deckard heard a dull song approaching, barely audible over the sound of the bane at the center of the crossroads.

He shifted his weight and lifted into the air between the treetops. He searched the forest floor and roadways for the source of the mystical music.

A band of at least ten armed bandits marched up the roadway from the lower parts of the valley. They were close to the crossroads, but none of them were charmed. If these men served the Suitor, they were under the influence of gold, not magic.

Deckard alighted on a thick tree branch to one side of the crossroads and waited for the bandits to approach.

Though the men only talked softly, their sprites and banes were clearly audible as they closed with the loud bane left by the Suitor to draw Deckard's sprites off his trail.

More than two-dozen bandits appeared. They sounded puzzled at not seeing anyone at the crossroads.

"Where is he?" asked one.

"The demon said he would be here," said a second.

"Damn beast tricked us," said another.

The second bandit shook his head, shifting snow from his black beard.

"Start searching. This is too good an opportunity to waste."

That one spoke as someone in charge. Deckard noted the man's fur cap and followed him with his eyes as the others fanned out around the crossroads. It would not take them long to find him in such a bleak environment. He waited on the branch, then reduced his weight to allow himself to drift off the limb and into the air.

A group of bandits heading his way saw him. They pointed and yelled. Deckard arced through the air over the crossroads. He glided, tending downward, over their heads. At ten hands above them, he restored his robe's full weight.

Deckard crashed down on top of two bandits. He flattened them to the ground.

The others screamed and thrust weapons at him. He deflected one blow from his face with an iron sleeve. The rest clanged ineffectually off his armor.

With a shove, he knocked the one he'd blocked to the snowy ground. The remaining three bandits before him retreated, wary of his next blow.

"Where is the demon?" he said, breath misting before him. "The Suitor?"

The bandits bellowed a roar and charged at him. Deckard turned blow after blow from his exposed head and hands. His sprites danced among the three bandits, until as one, they fell into a heap, tied together.

Deckard turned from his erstwhile attackers. He looked for the leader of the bandits but instead found ten more men rushing toward him as fast as the snow would allow along the roadway.

He ignored them and lifted into the air as they approached.

Gliding over the treetops, he spied the bearded leader and two of his men retreating along the opposite fork of the crossroads. Deckard aimed for the lead bandit and swooped down upon them.

A string sprite tripped one of them.

A blow from his fist felled the other.

He faced the leader, his expression full of dark intent.

"Damn it, no gold is worth this!" The bearded man shook with anger and fear. A dagger shook and then dropped from his hand to disappear into the snow.

"Where is the demon?"

"In the woods near here, a little house!" the leader blurted.

Deckard smirked.

"You can save yourself a blow if you lead me there," said Deckard.

The man grunted, his face pale with cold and fear.

"He'll do worse than kill me if I do."

"Of course, you must protect your life. How far to the house?"

"Not far." The bandit glared at Deckard. "But I won't go with you."

"No," Deckard said. "I can see that."

He brought his fist down on the man's skull. A crack resonated through the forest. The bandit leader crumpled, unconscious.

Hoofbeats approached from the road leading toward Keep Nothem. Bandits scattered into the forest as Saylese and her men at arms arrived on horseback. Saylese rode straight to Deckard, closely followed by her gray-haired sword servant and young parson.

"Deckard," she said, "is the Suitor near? Zadery?"

"No." Deckard scowled at the fallen form of the bandit leader. "But he sent these men to waylay us."

"What does the demon want with my son?"

"Most likely only leverage."

"No carnivorous proclivities, I dearly hope?" said the young parson Andrew Reen.

"He doesn't eat humans," said Deckard. "He sees you as the closest beings to him, even closer than other demons."

The parson paled, and his thin beard looked paler still with frost.

Jaska, Saylese's sword servant, frowned.

"Shall I order our men to round up these cowards?"

Saylese nodded to the older woman.

"Yes, but stay close." She turned to Deckard. "Did he tell you anything?"

"There is a house nearby in the forest. The suitor is using it as a hideout, so he may have returned there."

Saylese took the reins of her horse. The animal snorted hot breath.

Jaska barked orders to the men at arms. They sprang into action, rounding up the bandits unfortunate enough to remain nearby.

"Delegate to the sergeant," said Saylese to the sword servant. "You and Parson Reen follow me and Lord Hadrian."

"Yes, my lady," said Jaska and Andrew in unison.

Saylese looked down at Deckard from horseback.

"Lead the way, Deckard."

* * *

Three riders following below, Deckard battled the wind deeper into the valley. Odd, how he so often found himself afraid in the valley, but now, on the trail of a demon, he felt no fear within. He glided over trees and rocks and snowbanks. The horse's steps thundered after him.

The sky darkened, but Deckard released glowing string sprites to help the Saylese and the others keep him in sight.

His spiraling path cut in a greenish trail across the white clouds. A few miles from the crossroads, he spied the steeple of a sloped rooftop emerging from the trees. The building looked almost like a church of Mother Mercy, but smaller.

He added small amounts of weight, shifted the wind, and descended.

A thicket of trees with limbs covered in frozen ice crystals gleamed around the dark shape of the house. Deckard had expected a small cabin, but the house before him only appeared small from the outside.

Made of patterned black wood aboveground, the rest of the house was carved into the stone of the valley's wall. Shuttered windows with worn sills stood out as pale spots in the dark walls of the house. Deckard swooped low and landed on the house's slanted rooftop. He looked back toward the others as they broke through the tight circle of trees and into the clearing around the house.

Saylese gazed around the clearing.

"I had no idea at all there was a building here."

Deckard glided down to them from the rooftop and floated in the air.

"Neither did I... I have spent little time in the valley in recent years."

"Do you think it is a new construction?" asked Andrew.

"No, but it is well hidden," said Deckard.

Saylese shivered visibly.

"The demon is inside, we must take our chances to save my son."

"I agree." Jaska drew the lesser of the two swords she wore at her waist, leaving the dire blade she carried as Saylese's sword servant in its sheath.

Deckard nodded.

"You're right."

"Parson Reen," said Saylese, "please use your magic to protect our rear."

"Yes, my lady." Andrew bowed his head.

"Jaska, give me my sword."

The older woman obeyed. She unsheathed Saylese's dire blade, its edge shimmering but its side black as a starless night. Saylese took the sword and rode to the front steps leading from the snow to the covered porch before the doors of the house. She stepped onto the porch. Deckard landed at her side.

"The fight will not be easy," he said.

"I am able to use my sword, Deckard," she said.

"That is not my concern. I fear the Suitor will harm Zadery."

"We cannot stop that unless we attack."

"True," he said and masked his doubts in confidence as Jaska and Andrew caught up with them. "Let us enter."

Jaska nodded. Andrew bowed his head and the song of his trained sprites and banes intensified, though it would remain inaudible to those lacking the gift to hear it. Saylese faced the door, her fingers tight on the grip of her blade.

Deckard pulled one of the double doors to test it. The door opened easily, unlocked.

His eyes narrowed as Deckard guessed the Suitor would not be alone. Surely, he would have more minions.

An arrow embedded in the door frame beside Deckard. He stepped back in surprise. Torchlight within illuminated a dozen armed bandits with similar sprite songs to those at the crossroads. There were differences, however.

Arranged in two rows, they looked ready for a fight. Six in the rear carried bows and quivers of arrows. Six in the front bore shields and wore dull shining breastplates along with swords. Not bandits, then, Deckard realized, but more likely professional mercenaries from a nearby city.

Between the two lines, huddled the shaking form of Zadery, hunched and sitting on the floor.

"Zadery!" called Saylese.

Deckard scowled at the mercenaries.

"Stand aside."

"He warned us you'd be here," said a scar-faced man with a black scarf wrapped around his neck over a high, collar of armor. "Hadrian. But tell me something. Do you know who I am?"

"Should I?" Deckard said. "Mercenaries fight and die every day, so I don't pay them much heed."

"You are a fool, Hadrian," said the man. "I once served with her holy Order of the Smoke. My name then was Sir Richard Thornasa."

Saylese took a step forward. "A former knight? Why do you serve the Suitor?"

"Tell her ladyship for me, Hadrian. I think you know." Richard smirked. "Unless you've forgotten what you did."

"If you want revenge for a master you never knew then you're ten tenths a fool." Deckard shook his head. "Lay down your weapons and I will forgive you, Thornasa."

"It's not I who needs forgiveness, Hadrian. Confess your deeds!"

Deckard glimpsed Andrew and Jaska exchanged glances of confusion, their movement reflected in Richard's polished round shield.

"I'd not ask for your pardon, Thornasa. Nor for your old master's."

Richard's scar curved into the corner of his mouth as he snarled.

"Then let steel settle the grudge, prince of glass."

Richard fell back behind the other five swordsmen. He grabbed Zadery by the shoulder and dragged him to his feet.

"Unhand my son!" Saylese charged forward, weapon readied.

Her dire blade clanged against the steel shield of one soldier, its black edge denting the metal, but with its invested magic inactive it did not cleave the steel as Deckard knew its kind were capable.

Passed down among the founding families after the Conquest, dire blades could cut through any material to harm the target of its user's rage.

Deckard matched his pace with Saylese's charge.

His iron sleeve intercepted a blade aimed for her. He batted aside the mercenary's shield with the same arm. Deckard's open hand found the man's throat.

Fingers tightened.

The swordsman struggled.

Deckard lifted him off his feet without using his sprites to take the man's weight. His muscles protested with pain at the twenty stone or more lift in one hand.

The other four swordsmen retreated.

The archers took aim at Saylese and Deckard.

His sprites took some weight from the struggling man in his grip.

Deckard hurled the mercenary at the archers as if he was a bolas.

As the man left Deckard's grip his mass returned to him, adding to his momentum. His form spun and caught two of the archers at waist-level. They went down under his armored weight.

Richard Thornasa raised his head where he had ducked.

"Clever trick, Hadrian."

"All too kind." Deckard grimaced as he clashed with a pair of fresh mercenaries.

To his left, Jaska and Saylese each took on a single opponent.

The remaining archers regrouped and took aim at the unarmored women.

Andrew Reen's chanted incantations were joined by a chorus of bane song from within him. A gust of warm wind, as if from the southern sea stopped all four arrows in flight and blew them to the corners of the room.

The archers retreated, reaching for new arrows, seemingly unimpressed.

Their nervous expressions betrayed their true lack of confidence.

Deckard blocked one man's sword with his sleeve. The other mercenary's blade deflected off his robe's collar.

That was a near miss, Deckard thought in annoyance. He tripped the second swordsman with a sprite string. With a flick of his wrist, he sent another string to bind the man to the floor.

The sword he had just parried fell from its wielder's hand and thudded to the wooden boards at their feet.

Deckard shook his head as his erstwhile attacker retreated toward the line of archers.

"Your men are as brave as you, Thornasa."

Deckard stalked toward the former knight.

Richard pushed Zadery behind him, toward the archers.

The young boy stumbled to a stop in front of the shaken mercenaries.

Richard extended his sword toward Deckard's chest. His eyes gleamed with fury and he held his shield at chest height.

"I'll fight you, Hadrian. Man to immortal. Come at me."

Behind him, the swordsman fighting Saylese cried out in pain, then fell.

Richard gritted his teeth and lunged at Deckard.

They clashed back and forth a few times, the silver-edged sword sweeping into iron-hard sleeves.

When Deckard retaliated with sprite strings, Richard weaved away and avoided entanglement.

"You certainly fight better than your men," Deckard said.

Richard snarled, in reply rather than rejoin with words. His breath came fast from his scarred mouth. Sweat ran down his cheeks from his armored cap.

Deckard darted to his right. Richard followed him, his blade stabbing for Deckard's chest.

His robe proof against such strikes, Deckard sent sprite strings toward Richard's shield-arm. The man followed through with his thrust while the glowing strings wrapped his arm to his side.

The tip of his blade continued forward, its edge blurring into billowing smoke.

Deckard realized too late the man had learned more tricks than mundane sword skills in the Order of the Smoke.

Richard's blade became as untouchable as smoke. He released the grip and the weapon drifted upward. It reformed at a level just below Deckard's brow.

In his instant of realization, Deckard reeled back.

The blade slashed a thin line across his forehead.

He only barely avoided losing an eye.

Deckard brought his arms together and caught the sword between his sleeves.

The blade hung where he caught it. He lowered the weapon to the floor.

"Clever trick," Deckard said as blood trickled from the cut above his right eye. He took the hilt of the sword and faced Richard.

The former smoke knight drew a dagger from his belt.

"The fight is not over, Hadrian," he rasped, fighting for breath and struggling with the shield bound to his left side. He glared at Deckard. "I won't give up."

Saylese's dire blade stabbed into Richard's right shoulder.

Richard screamed and dropped his dagger.

Deckard kicked the weapon behind him and lowered his blade.

"You may as well," he said.

Another blast of hot air from Andrew's magic stopped the next flight of arrows.

Jaska dropped the last mercenary swordsman.

Richard looked around him, face contorted in fury.

"I'm not done. You won't win."

Deckard glanced at Saylese.

She nodded to him.

His right cross struck Richard in the chin. The former knight crumpled.

Saylese raised her dire blade.

"Surrender, and you will be spared," she said to the few mercenaries still standing.

Four bows and four quivers clattered to the floor.

Saylese lay the flat of her blade across her shoulder.

Zadery ran to his mother.

"Are you alright?" she asked him.

Zadery nodded.

"Where is the demon?" Saylese asked.

"I don't know," said Zadery.

Jaska went among the mercenaries, collecting their weapons.

Saylese turned to Andrew.

"Send a sprite as a messenger to the crossroads. Our dungeons will be full tonight."

"At once, my lady."

She extended her dire blade hilt-first to Jaska as the sword servant dropped a collection of bows, arrows, and blades in sheathes at Saylese's feet.

The gray-haired swordswoman replaced the dire blade in its scabbard at her waist. Deckard smiled at the thought of how fluid Saylese had been in using the weapon.

She raised her eyebrows at him.

"Is something amusing?"

"It is good to see a dire lady with skills in her ancestral weapon."

"I told you before, I trained as a knight," she said with a small smile. "But I see you need no blade of your own."

He shrugged.

"Lucky for this man."

His toe nudged the boot of the unconscious Richard Thornasa.

Saylese nodded.

Andrew returned from outside the doorway.

"My lady, the men at arms should be here at once."

"Good," she said.

Heavy steps announced the arrival of what could have been a horse outside if the sound had been a little lighter. Deckard frowned because he knew that sound belonged to no animal.

Virgil Silas Dane appeared in the doorway beside Andrew as Deckard and Saylese turned in his direction.

"Lady Nothem," said Virgil in a harsh voice. "The Suitor has attacked the keep."

Saylese scowled.

"The kidnapping was a distraction."

Deckard nodded, his stomach heavy with dread.

The Crimson Suitor liked to prepare himself a room where he would take his brides. Cold filled Deckard as he considered what the demon was planning.

"We must return at once," said Saylese. "I will not have that craven thing sit upon my throne."

Jaska and Andrew bowed their heads.

"Your horses are still outside," said Virgil. "Ride hard, before he can close the gates."

"He won't close the gates," said Deckard. "I see a plan."

"Parson Dane," said Saylese, "stay here until my men arrive. Watch over my son."

"As you like," said Virgil with a tip of his broad-brimmed hat.

"Deckard, you are with me," said Saylese.

"Of course, my lady."

"Then let us ride," she said.

* * *

Deckard took to the air just after the horses. He did not miss the fact that Saylese had been watching out for him by leaving Virgil behind. The old parson could turn on Deckard at any moment if his master commanded it.

Wind carried Deckard toward Keep Nothem.

Saylese had touched his hand when they first met. Deckard wondered if she meant more than to sway him to stay by such contact. His mission remained the same, but the more he saw of the widowed lady, the more he cared for her.

All the more reason to hurry, he thought.

As he neared the walls of the keep, a stiff counter wind hit Deckard, slowing his progress. He scowled and climbed in altitude, trying to find a way over the air current, but the wall of air continued a full half-mile up.

Circling around to try again, Deckard heard a bane song on the wind.

Of course, he thought, the Suitor is trying to stop me from reaching the keep with the others. Most likely he charmed a local hedge mage to alter the weather.

The dark forest below was impervious to his sight, but Deckard followed the song of the spirits gradually toward the ground.

After ten minutes of searching, he found the mage, a young man, probably still an apprentice, shivering in the cold of the night. The mage stood just beyond the wall of wind.

Deckard landed, then pressed through the darkness toward the young mage. In the darkness, the mage did not see him until he stood just ten hands away.

"Cancel your spell," Deckard called through the wind blustering around him. "This is over."

"It is," said the young man with a grimace of concentration on his face. "You will arrive too late, demon hunter."

Deckard pressed forward.

The mage laughed out loud.

"The Suitor will reward me once he has bedded his bride."

Deckard loomed over the youth.

"If you believe that, you're as much a fool as the demon you serve."

His fist found the man's jaw in the midst of the wind.

The hedge mage fell to his knees, then collapsed into the snow. His breeze banes retreated into him, and the counter wind died. Deckard glared at the unconscious form. Without the wind on his side, the mage could be right. Deckard gritted his teeth and took to the air.

Saylese and the others must have arrived by now.

He prayed they would wait for him before entering the gates.

* * *

He approached Keep Nothem from above, the wind at his back and in his ears. Flakes of snow swirled all around him as he circled lower.

A few guards patrolled the parapets, all of them bound to the Suitor by the dissonant songs of charm-banes. Deckard spotted no horses anywhere inside or outside the walls. He did not dare hope Saylese and the others had waited.

Flying low over the walls, he aimed for the door of the keep he had used when he first arrived. The same guard he had lent his gloves stood watch, but a charm-bane hummed within him.

Deckard's sprite strings tripped the guard before the man could even reach for a sword. Deckard crouched beside him, stifling a warning cry with one hand. Another string reached into the man's mind and withdrew the bane the Suitor had left there to charm him. Deckard released the demon's bane, then took his hand from the guard's mouth.

"My Lord, forgive me," he said.

Deckard shook his head.

"Let me inside. Quiet as you can."

The man bobbed his head. He opened both doors.

"Stay here and make sure none of the other guards get past you," said Deckard.

"Lady Nothem is already inside," said the guard.

"As I feared," murmured Deckard.

"Her parson and sword servant are with her."

"I doubt they will be enough on their own." Deckard brushed past the guard and into the entryway behind him. "Good luck."

"You also, my lord." The guard gripped the hilt of his sword with one of Deckard's gloves.

Deckard gave him a nod, then slipped into the keep.

* * *

In the otherwise-deserted seat hall, he found Saylese, Andrew, and Jaska. Saylese turned as he entered. She saw Deckard first.

"Deckard," she said, "what kept you?"

"The Suitor enlisted a hedge mage. He delayed me."

"I'm glad you're alright."

"Likewise," said Deckard.

Jaska frowned.

"Where is everyone?"

"If the Suitor charmed them, who knows?" said Andrew.

"I'm afraid you'll find out soon enough, servants," said the Crimson Suitor as he stepped out from behind the glimmering dire throne.

He smiled at Saylese from behind the bars of his helmet.

"I have plans for us, dear lady."

"Hold your tongue, demon," she said.

The Suitor tapped the ruby pommel of a sword sheathed at his belt.

"I'm afraid I cannot obey, my dear." He paced to stand before the throne. "So long as I stand here, I promise you will be mine this night."

"To the pit with you," she said.

"Oh, my dear, you wound me." The Suitor's smile slipped away. He turned his red eyes to Deckard. "Don't be taken in by the words of the demon hunter. He would see me thrown down a world well rather than embrace you." His lip curled. "But remember, he has never bested me before."

"This time is different," said Deckard.

"On this, we cannot agree, Hadrian." The Suitor's smile broadened once again. "But I know you find Saylese as intriguing as I... Only fitting, as this time I will see you dead for interfering with my plans."

"Go ahead then," said Deckard, extending one hand, palm up. "Test your blade against my abilities."

"Perhaps later," said the Suitor. He raised the hand not resting on the pommel of his sword. Holding out in a gesture similar to Deckard's, the demon snapped his fingers.

From the doors positioned on both sides all along the room, a mob of charmed servants, guards, and villagers rushed into the seat hall. The song of their banes dazzled Deckard's hearing with a dissonant cacophony. They swarmed the center of the room and the only four people not under the command of the Suitor.

Gusts of wind forced a few back, but Andrew's incantations quickly lost their strength as the Suitor's mass of banes drowned out his commands to his own inner spirits.

Jaska reached for her sword but Saylese held out a hand to stop her.

"Stay your blade. These are our own people, Jaska."

"So noble," said the Suitor. "My dear, that is why I love you."

"You cannot love me, demon. You don't even know me."

"Oh, but I know you." The Suitor sounded indignant. "I have studied you, my bride to be. I have listened to tales of your sorrow, of your dedication to your fallen husband. I have heard of how you dismissed other knights who tried to comfort you in your grief, how you have not let any man touch your body or your heart since his passing. You can swear off the love of mortals, my dear, but you cannot deny my devotion."

"Devotion? You violate women and call that love? Is that it, demon?"

The Suitor grimaced.

"You will see the truth in my words, Saylese."

She glared at him.

"How can an immortal demon speak so foolishly? Have you lived at all in your millennia of existence, Suitor?"

"I have a name, Saylese. And when I whisper in your ear afterward, you will know I am no fool."

"I will never let that happen," she said, teeth clenched.

"Say that if you wish," said the demon. "Your people will deliver you to me." He snapped his fingers again.

The mob rushed at the four of them from all sides.

Jaska released the belt of her sheathed sword, but kept the weapon blunted in its scabbard. Her first blow sent a man sinking to the floor, clutching his knees.

Deckard lashed out with sprites and fists. He threw charmed people to the floor with every string and every blow.

Reen sent blasts of focused air to hammer attackers back from Saylese, who tripped some and pushed others back as the four of them retreated through the seat hall toward the doors where Deckard had entered. Before they could reach the exit, another wave of armed guards under the Suitor's charm appeared from a side-passage and blocked their path.

The Suitor followed them down the steps of the throne and across the seat hall.

"You will not leave here before you accept me, beloved."

Saylese grimaced. She turned from the last villager she had thrown to the ground faced the Suitor.

"I will not repeat myself again. Never will I be your bride."

"The choice is not yours," said the Suitor. "Love demands reciprocation."

Deckard grunted.

"She said no, demon." He drew out two piercing banes and wrapped the end of a sprite string around each one, deftly so the lethal banes would precede the glowing strings in flight.

He stood beside Saylese and prepared to strike.

Then came a shriek of air being rent apart, followed by the sound of thunder. The guards at Deckard and Saylese's backs fell to the ground, clutching at their ears.

Virgil stepped into the seat hall and began picking his way over the fallen men, who still twitched with paralyzing static charge.

"Forgive me for the delay, Lady Nothem," he said.

The Suitor stared at him.

"Who are you, old man?"

"I am Parson Virgil Silas Dane, servant of the Clan of Geteren and its master, Lord Cyrus Bode."

"Tell Bode that, like his brother, no agent of his will ever best me." The Suitor raised his voice. "Leave now or die, mortal man."

Virgil arched one eyebrow. "Ever arrogant, aren't you, Crimson Suitor?"

"Kill the servants, my friends," said the Suitor. "Bring Saylese to me."

Charmed people staggered to their feet. They surged forward, renewing the attack.

Deckard's sprite strings tripped one cluster of people from the Suitor's charmed mob. Virgil roared an incantation. Cold wind from blew open the high windows and formed a storm of ice and glowing ethereal flower petals in the mass of humans. Virgil's spell floored the mob as one.

Saylese leaped over the fallen servants and villagers, followed by Jaska and Andrew. Deckard raced at her side.

The Crimson Suitor faced them beyond his broken human wall.

"That's it," murmured the demon. "Come to me, beloved."

Saylese snarled.

"Don't call me that." She motioned to Jaska. "My sword!"

Jaska drew the gleaming black length of the dire blade from the second sheath at her belt. She deftly reversed the weapon and handed it to Saylese hilt first.

"A privilege few ever get, to witness a beauty such as you draw a weapon in passion," said the Suitor.

"Shut up," hissed Saylese.

"My dear, such fire becomes you!" said the Suitor.

"Be careful," said Deckard. "He's trying to goad you."

"I can see that," said Saylese through clenched teeth.

The Suitor's eyes never left Saylese.

"Hadrian," he said, "you should know I would not insult my bride, however willful she becomes. What I say is only the highest compliment I can conceive at the moment."

Saylese glared at the Suitor, positioning herself and her dire blade in a tight, guarded stance.

"If you want me, demon, come and get me."

"If you wish, my dear."

The Suitor bowed with a flourish of his arms. Bright wings spread on his back. He drew the long sword with the ruby pommel. His knees bent as though preparing to leap forward.

Saylese held her black sword steady.

Deckard tensed to intervene once the Suitor charged. He would not let the demon fight Saylese one on one.

The Suitor called out in a high-pitched voice, "it is time!"

He launched himself through the air toward Deckard, Saylese, the sword servant, and the young parson.

Jaska stepped forward, blade cutting toward the Suitor's wing.

The demon twisted his path out of range. A trio of banes flew from his outstretched hand and darted toward Jaska. Deaf to magic, the sword servant had only seconds to see the tiny lights. Her eyes glazed over.

Deckard shouted a warning, too late.

The demon beat his wings and sailed over Deckard and Saylese. He narrowly avoided a flurry of Deckard's sprite-strings. Saylese whirled and cut at the demon.

The Suitor landed just out of reach, beside Andrew. Though the demon's blade was bare, he shot three more banes at the parson. Andrew's eyes grew hazy, then cleared.

Saylese interposed herself between the Suitor and her young parson.

"Are you alright, Andrew?" she asked.

"Fine," he said and shook himself.

Jaska did the same.

Deckard's eyes narrowed. The bane songs from within each of them were the same as the others now. He darted between Saylese and Andrew.

"He's charmed them, Saylese."

"Quick one, aren't you?" said the Suitor.

Deckard faced Andrew. Jaska turned toward the rest of them. The Suitor paced stepped backward, pacing away from Saylese.

"In time, your people become mine," he said.

Saylese grunted and pressed her back against Deckard's.

"If we defeat the demon, you can restore them like the others. True?"

"True," he said, his mouth dry.

She took a deep breath.

"Then do not hurt them badly, Deckard."

"Yes, my lady."

Jaska took up a fighting stance between Saylese and the Suitor. Andrew began to chant, his eyes on Deckard.

Saylese gave a heated battle cry. She clashed with Jaska, black dire blade ringing off polished steel behind Deckard's back.

Deckard drew out a set of sprite strings and lashed at Andrew. The young parson avoided some with swift steps and turned away a few that got too close with a counter-magic chant.

The Suitor laughed, high and shrill.

Deckard grimaced and pressed forward against Andrew.

A gust of wind buffeted Deckard. Thanks to his robe and body becoming as heavy as he needed, he remained rooted in place.

He lunged for the parson, hoping Virgil would not seize the opportunity to strike him from behind. At least the old man wasn't charmed and attacking as well.

One of Deckard's sprite strings wrapped around Andrew's legs. He swayed as Deckard pulled the loop tight. The young parson fell to the floor.

Deckard turned to see Saylese forcing Jaska back step by step toward the Suitor.

A low chant came from behind Deckard.

"Damn, stay quiet," he said, turning to face the prone parson.

Andrew completed his incantation. A focused jet of red fire leaped from his palms and shot toward Deckard.

His armored robe could not keep heat out.

Deckard knew how it felt to burn.

"Not this day."

He darted to the side and circled Andrew, closely followed by the billowing fire sweeping in an arc at chest level.

Deckard drew close. He delivered a kick to Andrew's chin. The parson reeled back. His bane-sparked fire vanished in an instant. The song of his inner spirits went soft as he fell unconscious.

Suppressing a sigh of relief, Deckard turned toward the Suitor.

"You know I hate fire," he said.

"All too well, demon hunter. Fire is like love, so it stands to truth you would despise it."

Saylese's dire blade rang against Jaska's one last time. The lesser sword broke in two pieces, cracking halfway along its blade. Jaska stumbled backward, defenseless. Deckard and Saylese faced the demon.

"Don't listen to him, Deckard."

He nodded, eyes on the demon.

"If either of us understood human love, I'd let you fly away right now." Deckard smirked. "But this is a dire keep, so there is a world well just beyond the south wall, and I'll hurl you down it before sunrise."

The demon snarled wordlessly, then spat on the floor between them. Deckard glanced at Saylese, but she did not meet his eyes. Her gaze remained fixed on the Suitor's tall helm, the bars that halfway hid his face, and the flickering red eyes behind them. She unclasped the cloak about her shoulders.

She leaped at the monster, her long winter cloak billowing across the floor behind her. The dire blade she wielded in both hands slashed at the demon's face. Saylese yelled in rage as the Suitor's ruby-pommeled blade intercepted her weapon's black edge.

Both weapons held.

Saylese bounded backward, out of reach of a counterattack the Suitor did not even attempt. The Suitor's lips curled, barely visible beyond his barred mask.

"Truly, a beautiful blow," he said, looking down at the length of his silvery sword. A gleaming notch carved into the demonic steel where Saylese had struck. The Suitor's eyes locked with hers. "I knew you could be the one, Saylese."

Bane songs grew louder as the Suitor's voice trailed off. He gazed at Saylese, expression bright and smug. Three banes danced from each hand. The six banes encircled Saylese.

She jerked back, trying to escape the wisps of darkness.

Deckard lunged forward.

"No, you won't have her!"

"I won't be stopped, demon hunter. Not by you, nor by the old wizard at your back."

The Suitor's banes encircled Saylese, then pressed her from every side. She swung at one with her blade, but the weapon was too coarse an instrument to cut something every mage knew had as much substance as air.

Saylese went stiff. Her blade extended in her hand, frozen after the last swing. She sagged slightly, eyes clouding over.

"Virgil," said Deckard. "Don't turn against me."

"My goal and yours are the same," said Virgil, "this time."

"Humans will always fail in the face of love," said the Suitor. "Mortal or immortal, you know nothing of elemental truth."

Out of the corner of Deckard's eye, he saw Virgil raise one fist, then unfold his hand. He saw the gesture Virgil intended.

The Suitor beat his wings and took to the air, making torchlight dance and sputter. The demon flew toward Virgil.

"No spell will delay my love!"

Deckard lunged under the demon and toward Saylese.

The Suitor's notched ruby blade thrust at Virgil. The old mage laughed as he ducked the strike.

Deckard knew why.

The gesture Virgil had made was rude, but not magical, yet he had fooled the Suitor into attacking him, rather than fleeing with Saylese.

Deckard tackled Saylese about the mid-section. They tumbled to the floor, her beneath him, arms pinned by the weight of his heavy robe.

"Coward!" roared the Suitor.

Virgil continued to retreat, using static electricity in his bolt gloves to jolt each of the demon's strikes off course.

"I'll say this for Hadrian," said the wizard, "he's not as predictable as you, demon."

The Suitor bellowed in rage. The gusts from his wings extinguished multiple torches as he turned to fly toward Deckard.

Warm beneath him, Saylese scowled.

"Let me go, Deckard. He won't hurt me."

"You're charmed. And the Suitor is called crimson because his brides don't survive the wedding night."

"I'm not like the others. He thinks the same thing."

"Of course he does. He's influencing you."

"It doesn't feel that way, Deckard. Please."

"Saylese, I'm here to protect you."

Eschewing his blade, the demon barreled into Deckard from behind. Despite his robe, the impact knocked the wind out of Deckard. The Suitor hurled him against the wall, rattling the flickering torch in its bracket overhead.

The Suitor lifted Saylese, then tossed her over his shoulder. She left the dire blade on the stone floor.

Deckard sank to his knees, breathing painfully and fast.

"Goodbye, demon hunter," said the Suitor. "This night is mine, and my bride's."

The demon turned and marched from the hall.

Another wave of charmed villagers and servants converged on Deckard and Virgil.

Deckard picked up the dire blade, then found his feet.

Electricity and cries echoed along the seat hall.

Deckard regained his composure as he and Virgil broke through to the tower staircase where the Suitor had taken Saylese.

He hoped they were not too late.

* * *

He raced up the stairs, body light, feet heavy. His boots drove against stone. Virgil's winded gasps were audible behind him but Deckard had no thoughts left for the wizard. The Suitor had Saylese, and if Deckard did not catch him now, he might never, would never, stop the demon. His motivation had never been stronger.

Deckard stormed to the top of the steps, well ahead of Virgil, who sounded as though he might be two floors down.

He threw open the door to a warmly furnished bedchamber. The Suitor stood before him, lips trembling, silver blade bare in his hand. Saylese sat on the side of the bed, framed between two curtains. Her face was pale and flecked with sweat, and her eyes cloudy.

"What do you want, demon hunter?" the Suitor said. "Why fight to keep me from my bride?"

"Demon, you've never let one of your brides live through the night."

The demon scowled.

"I did not expect you to understand, but..." His lip curled. "I thought you'd spout some of Mercy's dogma."

"I've studied your pathology, demon. It appears you have not had the opportunity to do the same for me."

"Hadrian, you've never lived in the caverns, never dwelt in darkness. You are favored by She who dwells above!" The demon hissed. Spittle flew onto the rugs covering the floor. "You are a pampered creature and a beast of burden for Mother Mercy. I doubt a single question for her has ever arisen in your head."

Deckard shook his head.

"You really don't know anything about me, after...what, five battles before?"

"Small change for one of my kind," said the Suitor.

"The well waits for you, demon."

"D-don't..." Saylese's voice sounded weak, frail, unlike her.

The demon lunged at Deckard, sword stabbing at eye-level.

Deckard positioned himself behind the dire blade. He caught the Suitor's strike on the weapon's guard and shoved the demon back a step.

"You're stronger than me—Though only with your pathetic tricks." The Suitor pressed his attack.

Deckard caught the Suitor's third attack with the edge of the dire blade. He turned the strike so it sliced through one of the tapestries by his side. The demon retreated out of reach before he could retaliate.

The Suitor sneered.

"Just a trick. A trick. You're not swift enough to defeat me."

"I've beaten you before."

"Yes. Before." The demon's mouth twitched behind the cage of his helmet. "I have greater power now that I once did."

"Is that so?" Deckard said, "you might have fooled me to think otherwise."

The Suitor's brows bent and he glowered at Deckard.

"You mortals tell stories of ancient powers, but you know nothing of them."

Deckard cut at the Suitor's side. The demon darted back behind the bed frame, wary of the dire blade, despite Deckard's lack of experience with the weapon.

His silver blade thrust trough the curtains, visible only at the last second. The attack glanced off Deckard's high metal collar. The demon retreated again as Deckard circled around the foot of the bed in pursuit. On the other side of the curtains, Saylese shuddered enough to make the whole bed shake.

"Saylese," said Deckard, "stay there."

"Deckard..." she sounded tearful. "...he—he won't let me."

"Be still, my bride."

"Don't call me that."

The Suitor snarled and shoved his free hand through the curtains. Fingers closed on Saylese's shoulder while he faced Deckard.

"Faster or not, you are losing," said Deckard.

"You think this is all the ancients gave me?" roared the Suitor.

He withdrew his arm, dragging Saylese to his side.

Deckard hesitated, the dire blade poised in both hands. He kept his eyes on the Suitor, until he took a long glance at Saylese's face, shining with tears from the effort of resisting the demon.

"Don't look at her!" cried the Suitor.

Saylese met Deckard's.

"Destroy him. Please."

The demon screamed in fury. He clutched Saylese to his chest and closed the few hands-distance to reach Deckard. The point of his silver blade led the way. The demonic weapon rebounded off Deckard's armor twice, then gashed him just over the ear. The demon moved faster still, impossibly quick.

"Time is at my command," screamed the demon.

Deckard retreated under the rain of blows, only able to parry one of the last four to keep his head.

"You defy nature's order, demon hunter. Immortal." The Suitor seemed unburdened by Saylese as he followed Deckard toward the one window in the room, a high set with two sealed panes on the far side of the room from the bed.

Warm blood ran down Deckard's face from the gash by his ear. He placed himself behind the dire blade but removed one hand from the hilt. Parrying would fail him if he tried again, and he might lose his head next time.

Deckard put his back to the high window. He let his sprites take the weight of his robe, then the weight of his body. Sprite strings emerged from the fingers of his left hand.

"It is over." The demon seethed as he approached. "You will not live to witness my true marriage, Hadrian."

"It's certain, there will be no marriage tonight, demon."

The Suitor charged at Deckard. Wordless rage bellowed from his pallid lips. He delivered one strike toward Deckard's throat. Deckard turned the blade.

The Suitor's weapon darted toward the ear where he had cut Deckard before. In a frozen instant, the blade's edge cut into the previous wound. Deckard shot his sprite strings around Saylese's waist. He pulled her to him as he reeled backward.

Droplets of blood flew from the Suitor's blade. Deckard's head throbbed with deep pain. Red trickled before the flickering vision of his left eye. Saylese clung to him with warm arms. She held on even as he released her from the sprite strings.

The Suitor slashed at Deckard's head again. Deckard jumped backward. His robe met the window. For a second, he feared the lock would hold against his lack of weight, but with Saylese's added momentum, it failed.

The window crashed open. Deckard and Saylese sailed onto the frigid night wind. They sailed over the keep, caught in a slightly warmer updraft.

Saylese opened her eyes and gazed at Deckard. Shards of glass spiraled from her hair and gown and rained onto the tower rooftop below.

"Deckard," she said. "he almost had me."

She hugged him tightly. Her warmth drew out his curse. After a few seconds, as they remained in contact, armored robe or not, he felt the building darkness, the monstrous force within him. Not all immortals suffered from such a curse, but Deckard, as the Mother Mercy's chosen demon hunter, knew all too well the growing sensation.

Purity over love was Mother Mercy's dictate to her chosen warrior. Dedication over connection, Mother Mercy's punishment for past transgressions.

"Saylese," he cradled her to his chest, feeling gradually weaker and more vulnerable, feeling the passage of time. "It's too cold here. We must descend."

She gave a small nod. He added a tiny hint of his own weight, then guided the wind to lower them slowly toward the western wall of the keep. A shout rang out from the broken window of Saylese's tower room.

The Suitor unfurled his wings and took to the air. Deckard and Saylese glided to the snowy ground at the base of the western wall. While the pain remained from the doubly-cut place near his ear, Deckard sensed no further blood-flow. The curse did nothing to reduce his natural resilience.

They sailed over a wide, dark, well ringed on one side by the dark shapes of gnarled valley trees. Deckard knew as they landed nearby, this was no well for water. He recognized a world well by the soft dirge of the few sprites flitting along its edge and over its deathly pit.

We are so close, he thought.

To cast the Suitor down into the well meant victory, meant safety for Saylese. The realm of banished demons lay below in the darkness, and they never hesitated to drag a renegade who lingered within to join them in the depths.

The Suitor, undaunted by any risks he perceived, glided over the wall and flew toward Deckard and Saylese. The demon banked, then landed on the smooth-worn rim of the well on the opposite side from Deckard and Saylese.

"Stand away from my bride, Hadrian."

"Temper, temper." Deckard smirked at the Suitor. "After all, you don't want to exhaust yourself before you defeat me. Do that, and you'll only disappoint your new wife."

The Suitor's nostrils flared and he tensed to leap across the twenty-hands or more gap of the well. Deckard gently pushed Saylese back from him. He handed her the dire blade by the hilt.

"Ready to use this?"

"More than ready," she said under her breath.

He sensed no dissonance from her inner banes. She had defeated the Suitor's magic. Deckard faced the Suitor. His fingers spread apart, pulling strings from within him. His sprite-borne threads flickered in the gathering gloom.

"Are you going to stand there growling all night?" Deckard said.

The demon's wings fluttered, but he did not take to the air. The Suitor smirked.

"Joke all you want. Your death is certain. Now."

Deckard barely felt the edge of the dire blade as it sliced through the armor of his shoulder. Blood welled over the dark iron armor of his robe. Cold flashed in through the cut in the iron robe, chilling him.

He staggered to one side. Saylese circled past him to the edge of the well. Her eyes clouded over and the bane song in her spirit rang discordantly.

"Sorry," she said, tears in her eyes, "but he won't let me stand by while you fight him."

Deckard grimaced in pain. He shot a glare at the Suitor.

"You still have her under your control."

"You really ought to have looked deeper. No mortal can resist me." The Suitor grinned.

"Deckard..." Saylese dropped her voice to a near whisper, "get him now. I can't hold back much longer." The blade in her hands trembled.

"As you command," said Deckard.

He leaped toward the Suitor, strings shooting toward the demon.

The Suitor flew over the middle of the well to meet Deckard. The edge of his blade cut through the ends of two of Deckard's sprite strings.

Deckard's other bright strings encircled the demon's free arm. He glided past the Suitor, using the strings to turn in midair. Despite using most of his weight, Deckard's movement left the demon hovering, rather than pulling him off course.

The Suitor's sword slashed at his face. Deckard released his strings and glided to the side of the well, where he clung onto the inner wall, out of reach of the demon.

"You bore me, Hadrian," said the Suitor.

"Imagine that," Deckard said, between rapid breaths.

"After these past centuries, how does it feel...to be about to die."

Deckard grunted, fingers growing numb as he gripped the stone of the wall. He shifted his weight into his sprites. The Suitor turned toward him, sword gleaming in the chill air.

The blood pulsing from the wound on Deckard's shoulder ran hot. His eyes locked on the demon's sword arm. Threads lashed out from one hand. The blade moved to cut them apart with supernatural speed.

Deckard released his other hand from the wall. He drifted into the air, light as a feather. His second volley of strings shot toward the demon's arm, all five sprites seeking inward, holding a piercing bane at their fore.

The demon finished cutting through the fifth string from Deckard's other hand. None of those threads found purchase. Glowing lines streamed into the darkness of the well, casting shadows of misshapen things in the depths far below them. He glared at Deckard.

Deckard grimaced in reply. Three bane darts shot straight through the demon's forearm in different places. The other two hit the hand where the demon gripped his silver blade. Deckard tugged, dragging the demon's arm with him.

He pulled despite the increasing pain in his wounded shoulder, the numbness of his fingers, and the growing dizziness from his bleeding head.

The Suitor's sword twisted in his grip. He screamed in agony. The demonic blade ripped from his grasp and plummeted into the well. The demon's screams became a howl of rage.

"Don't be so mad. You'll follow your weapon in a moment." Deckard's teeth clenched.

"Hadrian." The demon flew toward him, his free hand forming a fist.

Deckard saw the blow coming. The fist passed over his head and thumped against the stone wall. He caught the demon's wrist and smirked.

"Say goodbye to the light."

Another set of threads entangled the Suitor's wings.

He released the threads and darts piercing the demon's sword arm.

The demon's breath blew hot against Deckard's face.

"You will not win."

Deckard grunted, all out of words. He hurled the Suitor down the world well. The demon bellowed and writhed, trying to break his wings free, as he tumbled into the abyssal blackness, where all rogue demons belonged beneath the earth. Deckard floated in the well, waiting for the screams to die away.

Before the Suitor's protests faded completely, another voice joined them.

Saylese screamed and dropped her dire blade to the ground. She hurled herself into the pit, drawn by the Suitor's controlling banes.

She fell past Deckard as he turned. He added weight, and dove after her.

Wind rushed on his face, warmer from below than it was above.

He folded his wounded arm to his side. He extended the other toward Saylese.

She looked up at him, eyes wide, limbs floating weightlessly in free fall.

He caught up a hundred hand-lengths down. Shadows clambered below, mouths hanging open. Demonic teeth and eyes glittered.

Deckard caught Saylese, one arm encircling her waist.

"He made me jump," she said. "I'm sorry."

Deckard nodded. He shifted his weight, then shot lines to the wall to slow his descent. At last, he flew toward the surface on an updraft, carrying Saylese with him. She looked at his face, her arms wrapped around him. He removed the Suitor's banes from her mind with a gentle tug of his sprite strings.

"You did it," she said. He set her on her feet beside the well.

He nodded again, truly weary for the first time all night. Usually, he did not tire but the curse broke that magic.

Saylese picked up the dire blade and let him carry her back into the air. He flew her to the tower window where they had crashed into the night. They landed in the darkened chamber.

She pulled the window closed, then walked to the bed. Her arms wrapped around herself. She shivered.

"You saved me," Saylese said, "after I stabbed you in the back."

"He made you do it. I don't blame you." Deckard followed her to the side of the bed.

Footsteps approached from the staircase below.

Virgil Silas Dane stepped out of the open doorway and bowed his head to Saylese.

"Lady Nothem, is the Suitor—?"

"Defeated." Saylese folded her arms and took a deep breath. She turned toward Deckard as she said, "thanks to Lord Hadrian."

"It was my honor to protect you, Dire Lady Nothem," said Deckard.

He did not intend to show it but was unable to keep the weariness from his voice.

"See to my people, please, Parson Dane. I feel the need to rest."

Virgil raised his eyebrows.

"My lady, the villagers and servants have recovered their senses."

"See that any we hurt receive assistance from the healers. And please, ensure my son returns to the keep safely."

"Of course, my lady."

Virgil bowed low and then swept from the tower room.

Saylese turned to Deckard. "Are you aware of the uses of the dire blade?"

A tingle of mending pain came from his shoulder, but the wound vanished, taking the pain it carried with it. Even the cut in his robe sealed completely.

"It can undo what it has done," said Saylese, "when the user wills it."

"Thank you," he said.

"No, it's you who deserves my thanks. Deckard, you fought for me. You saved me. I—You remind me of him..."

"Your husband."

"Yes. I'd say he always fought with honor, but that isn't true. He always fought for what we shared."

She walked the few steps to stand before Deckard. She pressed her head to his chest where the robe now hung open.

"I want you," she said. "You know that, don't you?"

His lips brushed through her dark hair in reply. She pulled herself against him, tighter than before.

"Please," she said. "I want to remember you as I remember him. As more than a warrior."

"If you wish."

"I do."

She reached for the collar of his robe, and with effort lifted the material to expose the thin cloth shirt beneath. He helped her, and the iron robe dropped to the floor. Deckard's hands found the strings of her riding coat. He unlaced them with ease, despite the darkness.

She kissed his throat, then his lips, then pulled the shirt over his head. The skin beneath the fabric was puckered and pale with countless long burn scars.

"What are they?" Saylese asked.

"The price of defying a greater demon," Deckard said.

"I won't ask any further." She stepped back from him, eyes on his face. "It must have been painful to live through once."

"You're right," he breathed.

Saylese dropped her riding clothes to the floor.

She touched his chest with one hand.

"Please, help me one more time tonight."

She guided him to the bed, then lay down naked before him. He followed her, pulling the curtains closed behind him.

They made love, slowly. With every moan and each gasp, he grew more and more tired.

When they finished, he slept beside her, feeling time passing even as he drifted off to sleep.

Yes, sleep, after more than ten years without, he found sleep. Only once, did he wake in the dark.

Saylese lay awake beside him.

"You changed, you know," she whispered, not reaching to touch him.

"I know," he said, "it is the way Mother Mercy lets me know my purpose."

"Your face...your manner. You are not one man, but two."

"I am one man. And one monster," said Deckard.

"So, in the end, I slept with a monster anyway." Saylese took a long breath. Tears beaded at the corners of her eyes.

Beads of sweat gleamed like tiny diadems on her brow.

"Not the end," said Deckard sadly. "Just one end of one night."

"You can rest. You need it now."

"You're right."

He drifted off, one arm around her, until morning.

Snow was still falling in the gray light before the day truly began.

He rose and dressed, pulling on his iron robe, it's surface cold in reproach of him. Saylese still slept.

Deckard walked to the window, opened it, and slipped outside. He let the wind take his feather-light frame and flew into the cold dawn, over towers, over ancient walls, over trees and rocks. He flew south, aiming to escape the storm.

Deckard Hadrian will return.


Look for Demon Scroll, the first full-length epic fantasy novel in the Demon Hunter series, available now as the start of the rest of the series.

Find      more      books      by      Tim      Niederriter      at mentalcellarpublications.com


Thanks for reading.

# Also by Tim Niederriter

Deckard's story continues in "Demon Scroll" Chapter One.

MELISSA

On the last day of the journey south, the weather reflected Melissa's nervousness. Winds died away like the gale in her heart while a sweltering sun rose. She marched beside the wagons and carriages, setting the pace for the other guards on foot. Her fragile plains-hat formed a ring at the peak of her shadow.

The heat wore on the caravan as it approached the orchards near the city. The climate of the southern riverland left Melissa wistful for a cold breeze. At the edge of the trees, she got her wish. Cool wind swept in from the east, smelling of the salt sea and the coastal algae of the Bay of Charin.

*Thank Mercy.* Perhaps a blessing was upon her today. They would soon reach the city where she'd been born. Melissa once left Soucot as a child and not returned until today. She'd departed as an exile, though a willing one. Today, she returned as one of Lady Nasibron's personally selected guards.

Melissa completed her prayer of thanks for the breeze as a shout went up from the front of the caravan. Word quickly passed along the line from the leaders at the forefront, to the main body, and then to Melissa's unit in the middle of the long train, where the nobility traveled.

Her friend Orm, a veteran guard of her unit, brought the message to her. His dark brows gleamed with sweat under the broad brim of his hat, a grassland shade similar to the one Melissa wore. "We are to stop at the Governor's Orchard," he said. "Tell the lady, if you may. I've learned she doesn't like men intruding on her."

Melissa nodded to Orm. "I'll take her the word."

He smiled. "I count on you too much lately."

"As long as you don't start to lean on me, big man."

His smile broadened. "Wouldn't dream of it. Thanks for jesting with my size and not my age."

"One must respect one's elders," said Melissa without cracking a smile. She turned toward the carriage where the lady and her niece rode.

Behind her, Orm chuckled.

Melissa smirked, but only when she was sure no one could see her. Seeming cold helped her avoid consideration as a woman in the caravan life. Melissa could be friends with Orm because he understood that fact. Most of the guards were young men, exactly who she would not want knowing she was anything but the best spear-fighter in the wagon train.

She found the lady's carriage. Melissa matched pace with the wheels, then knocked on the side-door. "Lady Nasibron, I have word from the head of the column."

The door opened a crack. "Well," said Lady Nasibron, an aging noble witch who sat on one side of the carriage's interior, "Out with it, girl."

"The caravan is stopping at the Governor's Orchard not far from here."

"We're close to Soucot," said Lady Nasibron. "Good. Good. I expect we'll meet with the governor presently, my dears." She directed the last sentence at the two younger women riding in the carriage with her.

"Of course, Lady Nasibron." The girl with Dominion-black hair inclined her head toward the witch opposite her. She made no motion or acknowledgment of Melissa at all. Melissa expected nothing more from any noble's daughter.

The other girl, one with nearly-white Palavian hair, folded her hands and then nodded to Melissa. "Thank you for the message." That was Lady Nasibron's sword servant, though Melissa did not remember the woman's name. She wore a dark cloak and carried a scabbard across her knees. A larger sword, the Nasibron family blade, was propped against the wall, almost as tall as its current wielder.

Melissa bowed her head, then retreated from the door and let the carriage pass. Her eyes followed the dark-wood conveyance and the four horses pulling it for a moment before she picked up the pace, hefting the spear strapped onto the travel-pack hanging from her shoulders. The cold wind escorted the caravan into the orchards around Soucot. She caught up with Orm.

"Did the witch snap at you?" he asked.

"Perhaps a little," said Melissa.

The plants on either side of the stone roadway were in bloom. Trees bore apples in all seasons in this place, kept by cycling gardeners who cultivated different breeds at different times of year. There was always fruit to harvest as a result. The book Melissa had been reading by the light of the campfires said the practice was centuries-old.

Her shift lasted through daylight and had been uneventful on the journey south. Most bandit groups wouldn't dare attack a caravan of their size, even if they didn't know a powerful witch and her sword servant were among the travelers.

If word of her traveling got around, Lady Nasibron's presence with them would likely be more a deterrent to raiders and brigands than any number of guards with spears and arrows. Melissa wondered if Orm had come to the same conclusion.

He breathed in deep, clearly savoring the southern air. His weathered face seemed younger, the lines less deep and pronounced now that they were truly in the region's grasp. Melissa was glad someone appreciated the warmth of this clime. After leaving Soucot, Melissa spent the rest of her young life up until recently forgetting the south.

The caravan came to a stop on the road beside the Governor's Orchard. Melissa's heart, for a moment rushed with excitement, even joy. She'd returned to the land of her birth. Those emotions quickly turned to dread as she thought of the possibility her parents might still live in Soucot. Melissa ought not to have to meet them again, given how they'd parted those nine years ago. Mother and father could forget her for all her concerns. She wished for a different life than the one they'd tried to push her toward.

Orm motioned to the bright, blue-painted roof of a pavilion down a stone walkway off the road. "That's the governor's shade if I'm not mistaken."

Melissa pointed with a finger as the shapes of people approached from the far side of the pavilion. A party of a dozen well-dressed members of the nobility surrounded a slim woman in a formal black gown.

"Governor Lokoth herself?" she asked.

Orm's eyebrows rose. "You may be right. See those two?" He indicated a pair of hulking men, both with skin a shade of light gray that blended to pale green. Shirtless, they flanked the woman in black, each carrying a heavy mace effortlessly, in one hand.

"I see them."

"They're demons," said Orm. "Members of the governor's forces."

"You're sure?"

Orm nodded. "I've seen men like that in the northlands too, in Wagewood, last I can recall."

Melissa had never seen a demon before. She frowned. "They look so human."

"Look closer. You'll see the demons' faces aren't like ours in shape, and they have ridges like horns over their brows."

Melissa squinted. "They're a hundred yards away," she said. "You have better eyes than mine, even at your age."

He shrugged. "I have to keep some kind of edge. Being sharp-eyed is practical, given our profession."

"I can't disagree."

Lady Nasibron's carriage rumbled to a stop near the path leading to the pavilion. The door opened, and the witch's sword servant descended the steps, using the hood of her cloak in place of a hat. She carried the small sword at her hip and the great sword on a sling over her shoulder in an ornate sheath and baldric.

After her, Lady Nasibron's niece, Elaine, climbed down. She wore a finely pleated skirt and a jacket of white over her maroon tunic. Elaine had spoken little to anyone outside the carriage throughout the weeks of travel. Melissa suspected Lady Nasibron would frown on her niece, a young noblewoman herself, consorting with the commoners.

When Lady Nasibron emerged from the carriage, she wore a dark hat and a smile that came with living every day for decades with a full belly. She joined her niece and her sword servant, then motioned to Melissa and Orm.

"You two, follow us. I won't let Governor Lokoth outnumber me by so much."

Orm glanced at Melissa, but she was already moving to join the three noblewomen. Any day she refused a simple request by someone so highborn was a day she risked her position. Orm followed her without further hesitation.

"You two are well on task," said Lady Nasibron. "Now stay at each flank. Aryal," she nodded to her sword servant. "Lead on."

Aryal threw back her hood, revealing long, bright hair. She marched up the path toward the pavilion. The other four followed her at Lady Nasibron's regal pace. No one rushed a lady with so much magical ability, evidently, not even an imperial governor of Jadiketz.

Under the shadow of the pavilion, dark-haired and dark-clad Governor Tandace Lokoth met them, leaving most of her party a few yards behind. She kept her demon bodyguards close. Did she fear the wizardess, or were the guards just part of the custom?

Melissa could not answer those questions, given her lower status. She'd studied many things in books, but the demons who served the governors throughout Tancuon were not among them.

"Lady Nasibron," said the governor in a smooth voice. "I've been eagerly awaiting your arrival."

"And grown older for it, I see," said the witch. "I take it you need me, or you would not have summoned me south by name."

"You think correctly," said the governor. "But before we discuss that matter, allow me to inform you of the other I requested who should be here shortly."

"You asked another wizard as well?" Lady Nasibron sniffed. "I'm insulted."

"Not just any wizard." Governor Lokoth smiled slightly. "I believe you're personally familiar with Deckard Hadrian."

Lady Nasibron stiffened visibly. "You'd summon that demon hunter here? At the same time as me? And you didn't think to mention that in your letter?"

"I hope there won't be a problem."

Nasibron snorted. "A problem? I daren't think you care about feelings, so in that case, nothing you would understand, Tandace."

Melissa's gaze followed the governor's expression as it changed from one of smug superiority, in knowledge and position both, to one of calculated coldness. That face Melissa knew all too well from looking into mirrors, from the polite smile to the chill in the eyes.

"You may tell me how you feel, Kellene," said the governor. "But in front of my people, you will call me by the title given to me by glorious Mother Mercy herself. You know what is appropriate. A learned wizardess such as you cannot claim ignorance."

"An impressive proclamation, governor. I meant only the offense you earned. Deckard Hadrian may be the greatest demon hunter who will ever live. Yet, he remains a man of questionable reputation. I will leave it at that."

Lokoth's lip twitched. Her face, still mostly free from aging lines in her forties, remained a mask of impassive and unemotional calm. Her eyes flicked to Elaine, where the dark-haired young woman stood at her aunt's side. "Girl, you are Palavian by descent, are you not?"

Elaine bowed her head. "As my mother before me, governor."

"Indeed. Your mother is an honorable lady, though I take it she does not practice magic as her sister here?"

"I fail to see the relevance of this, governor," said Lady Nasibron.

Melissa glanced at Elaine, whose face was reddening.

"Governor, my mother is having my aunt tutor me," said the girl.

"And your father? He is Palavian, is that not true?"

"Indeed, governor."

"Good," said Lokoth. "I take it you have studied the most common traits of the Palavian people, girl."

"Leave my student alone, governor," said Lady Nasibron, bristling visibly.

The demon guards stepped forward, each moving with precision, and no more than necessary. They made no gesture toward lifting their heavy steel maces. Aryal, the sword servant, tensed, stance going rigid. Melissa resisted the urge to reach for the spear hanging on her shoulder sling. Orm backed away a pace, clearly intimidated by the demons.

Governor Lokoth shrugged, raising both hands. "That's enough anger. I will honor your request this time, Lady Nasibron."

"Appreciated," said the old witch. "But I warn you. Don't push my student or me. Governor."

"Noted." Governor Lokoth sniffed the air. "I take it that goes for your guards too?"

"What would you have to say about my guards?" asked Lady Nasibron.

"Not much, I'm afraid," said the governor, smug smile once again curling her lips.

Orm made no response, eyes still on the demon guards. Melissa took a deep breath. *Too deep.*

"You," said the governor, pointing at her. "What is your name, guard?"

"I'm called Melissa."

"Your whole name," said the governor.

She bowed her head. "Melissa Dorian, governor."

Lokoth tapped her chin with a finger. "How long have you been in the employ of Lady Nasibron?"

"She's never employed me. I'm a member of the caravan guards she selected."

"Indeed?" Lokoth smiled, turning to Lady Nasibron. "You didn't even bring private troops?"

"I'm afraid not all of us have the same kind of resources as an imperial governor."

"It seems I was wrong to summon you from the Chos Valley. One mage, even one wizard, will not be enough to assist with my trouble."

"As you were equally vague in your letter, I must say, governor, this trouble of yours is still a mystery to me."

"And yet, here you are. The Magister's Guild will be displeased, but there is no helping that."

Melissa fought back a grimace. The mention of the guild stung, as the magisters had banished her from the south, those years ago.

Lady Nasibron laughed, not bothering to stifle or suppress the harsh sound. "I fear life in the valley is becoming boring, and for my student's health, I thought warmer weather would suit us both."

Lokoth's smile never dimmed. "On that, we can agree, Kellene."

"Tandace, it has been some time indeed." Lady Nasibron smiled, actually smiled, at the governor.

Melissa stared at the two women. Elaine's jaw went slack.

"Twenty-two years and perhaps a few days," said the governor. "When Mother Mercy chose me to govern."

"You made a terrible mage. The change has been for the best," said Lady Nasibron.

"I hope you're a better teacher now than you were then." Lokoth smiled. "Because I have a task for you along those lines."

"I already have a student."

"If I recall, you are more than capable of instructing multiple pupils at one time, Kellene. I wasn't your only student, last I saw you."

"I'm getting older, Tandace. And here you have summoned a mage with more experience than I if you need a tutor."

"Not a tutor. A drill instructor. And Hadrian refuses to fill that role if you must know."

Lady Nasibron sighed. "He still seems intent on taking his knowledge to the grave with him."

"I thought you hated the demon hunter?"

"Hate is too strong a word, but the man is bent on squandering what he has."

"Watch your words, Kellene," said Lokoth. "They say he can hear his name on the wind."

Lady Nasibron scoffed. "Nonsense. Such rumors mean nothing."

"I suppose you'd know better than I," said Lokoth. "can you train five mages in the arts at the same time?"

"I can, and have, trained more than that at once," said Lady Nasibron. "The question I think you should ask is how long such training will take."

"As quickly as you can," said the governor. "And as thoroughly."

"Tandace, you realize training quickly, and training thoroughly are opposed elements, like fire and water or sprites and banes."

"And yet, sprites and banes coexist in every mortal heart, balanced by the mind and spirit." Governor Lokoth smiled. "How long would you estimate before your students can be battle-ready?"

"Elaine," said Lady Nasibron. "How long have you been studying battle spells?"

"Two years, teacher."

"Are you ready for a battle, Elaine?"

"I'd ask not to be tested in one."

Lady Nasibron nodded. "And how long before you may study a sacra scroll?"

"Another year, at least," said Elaine.

"Correct. You see, governor, I agree with her. I won't push a student of mine into battle before he or she is prepared for it. To do so would be the utmost waste of time and energy."

"Is that so?" Lokoth shook her head. "What can you do in four months?"

"That depends on the students," said Lady Nasibron. "Those with clever minds and strong prior studies may pick up the skills fast enough to fight in that time."

Melissa's heartbeat grew louder in her ears. They were talking about training mages, maybe more than mages but wizards with the power to take on sacra forms. She stood still and attentive, enraptured by the conversation. To think, she'd been lucky enough to be called over by Nasibron out of sheer coincidence. Or was her placement another blessing from on high?

Clouds to the north parted, revealing the distant arc of the world's rings, the nearest of which gleamed brighter and a more metallic gold than the others. A warm draft rustled the clothes in the pavilion as the wind shifted.

"Perhaps we ought to search the skies," said the governor. "Hadrian may be due to arrive, given the way things are moving."

Lady Nasibron shrugged. "You remember some things from your studies, I see."

"You think too positively of my younger self," said Lokoth.

Lady Nasibron snorted in derision. "Obviously."

"Bring your people," said the governor. "Walk with me."

"You want to see him approach?"

"Of course. When I grew up, Hadrian's beauty and powers were legendary."

"Likewise," said Lady Nasibron.

The party followed the witch and the governor out of the pavilion into the hot light of day. Melissa and the others gazed at the bright heavens. Though they spoke of Deckard Hadrian, Melissa doubted she would see the immortal demon hunter in the sky.

In all of Jadiketz, only two men were said to live forever. Cyrus Bode of the Chos Valley, far to the north where the imperial capital once stood, was one of them. Deckard Hadrian was the other. In Melissa's books, she had read of others, but of the many who once claimed the gift of youth and life eternal, only two remained.

"There!" Orm pointed. "The lord of winds!"

The others, except for the impassive demon guards, crowded to him, following his gesture to the sky with their collective gaze. Melissa squinted against the light of the noonday sun. A gleaming speck of reflected light grew above them as the shape began to resolve. The form of a man grew clear as he approached. The man wore a robe of polished iron. The garment looked black against the sky but for glints of brighter metal on his shoulders and his wide belt.

How could he fly with such weight on his back and no wings? Melissa furrowed her brow. He was a mage, for certain, but she lacked the studies to say what one required to wield such an ability as flight.

As Hadrian drew closer, his long black hair flowed free behind him, rippling in the wind. He wore a sword at his side, sheathed in a black scabbard, and he carried a pack over one shoulder. At first, he seemed alone. Yet, as he reached the air over the pavilion, Elaine cried a warning and pointed to the sky above him.

A creature half-again Deckard's height dove toward him in near-freefall, leathery reptilian wings held close to a scaly humanoid body. The creature swooped toward the man in the iron robe.

"What is that?" asked Melissa.

"A vakari warrior." The governor's lips trembled. "Most likely that creature is trained in magic, as well. Get back, everyone."

The governor's party of hangers-on scrambled for the pavilion. Elaine and Aryal took Lady Nasibron and led her to the building, moving faster than Melissa guessed the aging witch could manage on her own.

Orm and Melissa brought up the rear with the two demon guards and the governor herself. Melissa hadn't gotten a positive first impression from Lokoth. Yet, the governor showed her nature in a crisis, springing to protect her citizens first.

The vakari warrior screeched an inhuman cry as Hadrian hurled it from the air. The reptilian creature struck the ground, not ten yards from where Melissa and Orm retreated beside the governor.

The lizard man roared, staggering upright. He loomed, over three yards tall, built thick in the upper body to support the pinions that until a moment ago held him aloft. Deckard Hadrian descended toward the aggressor, surrounded by the sound of unseen trumpets playing a divine symphony. The vakari warrior turned, eyes locking on the governor.

The reptile said no words, but the murderous intent evident in that gaze told Melissa everything she needed to know. The vakari wove a sign in the air, making a sound like chattering vermin. The demon guards lunged to fill the space between their mortal charge and the governor. Orm dove for cover behind one of the supports of the pavilion.

The song ringing from Deckard Hadrian grew louder as he raced toward the vakari. The creature beat his wings, hurling himself sideways on the breeze Hadrian rode toward it. The man in the iron robe hit the ground like a thunderclap where the dragon creature had stood. But the warrior already sailed overhead, flames dancing to discordant songs at the ends of his clawed hands.

"An attack spell," said the governor through clenched teeth.

Melissa stared as the vakari flew toward them, building the ball of fire in both hands.

Deckard turned and took to the air on another updraft that seemed to come from nowhere, but it pushed him in an arc away from the dragon man. He would be too late if the vakari hurled those flames. The reptilian warrior"'s eyes narrowed as he probably realized the same thing as Melissa.

With a rasping laugh, the lizard man hurled his magical fire at the governor. Melissa shoved Governor Lokoth to one side. The blast struck her, carrying not just the heat of a flame, but a weight like a huge bludgeoning fist. The world shattered like a glass mirror around her, and she flew backward into a beam supporting one of the pavilion's arches. The wooden column splintered. She fell to the stone floor, black spots swimming in her vision. She fought to breathe, to return some air to her lungs. Her spear's head clacked against the tile.

Yet, everything seemed alright somehow. Melissa lay on her side, her world moving gently, in falling fragments.

In one fragment, the demon guards raced to the governor's side.

In a second shard of consciousness, one filled with the sound of blessed music, Deckard Hadrian seized the towering vakari warrior by the throat. He lifted the creature with him in one hand as he took to the air.

In the next falling mirror glimpse, Melissa saw the vakari warrior crashed down in a broken heap.

The shards of perception hit the ground and the fragments began to fit together.

Orm and Elaine rushed to Melissa's side. Aryal, her small sword drawn, advanced on the fallen vakari. Deckard Hadrian's face appeared before Melissa. Then the world went dark.

# About the Author

Tim Niederriter, as you've no doubt gathered, write fantasy stories.

Tim is the son of two physicists from Pennsylvania, transplanted to Minnesota. His parents read him The Hobbit (repeatedly) at a young age. The math adds up. Tim fell in love with fantasy of all kinds. Diagnosed with an autism spectrum disorder at a young age, he immersed himself in fictional worlds his whole life. He studied fiction and literature at Gustavus Adolphus College and also has a strong interest in history and politics.

Tim co-hosts the roleplaying game podcast "Of Mooks and Monsters" and talks with other authors each week on his other podcast, "Alive After Reading."